GOLDEN MIST

VOL. 1
DAY OF THE CEREMONY

CONTENTS

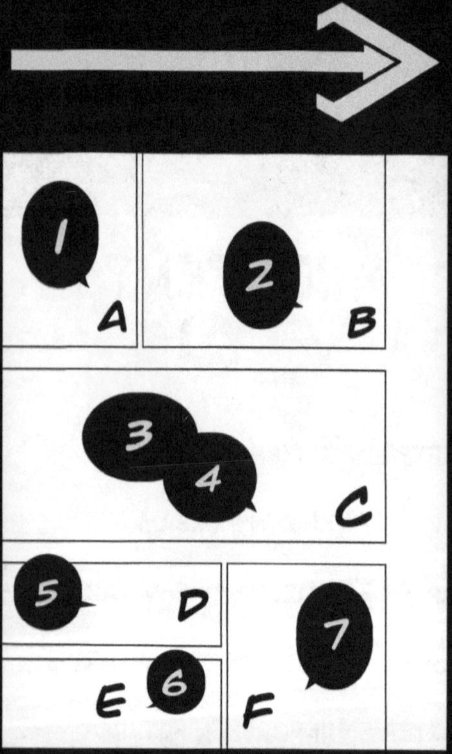

READ FROM LEFT TO RIGHT

GOLDEN MIST

VOL. 01
DAY OF THE CEREMONY

STORY AND ART BY
RED F MANGA

SHRINE COMICS Editorial
Jin Chan Yum Wai
DeAndre Moffett
Bree
Christian Sandino

Published by SHRINE COMICS

ISBN 978-0-6483217-2-9

KAI SORASHIMA

The descendent of Noshiba's number 1 hero! Ever since he was a child, he was raised by his grandfather to continue the legacy of his ancestor.

KAIZEN SORASHIMA

The leader of the Golden Mist and the hero of Noshiba, during the 16th century, he was beloved throughout the nation. however, things changed during the day of his ceremony.

JIKEN

A traveler stuck between time with a mysterious connection of Kaizen's fate.

🌀 ICHI

The vice captain of the Golden Mist clan. His goal is to make everyone see the meaning behind Kaizen's dream.

🌀 RAIDEN

The Golden Mist's tank and hardhead. Despite his fiery temper, his unmatched speed and animal instincts become stuff of legends

🌀 SIYKU

The chief strategist for the Golden Mist, wielding the shadows as his weapon with silent prowess.

🌀 HINA

The weapons expert of the Golden Mist, proficient in combat, stands as a formidable presence on the battlefield.

🌀 YIRI

The illusionist of the group. Despite her bubbly personality, Possesses the most frightening ability.

Embarking on this journey with my series "Golden Mist" has been a dream come true. While it may not fit the typical manga mold, My goal is to transcend the medium and create a story that resonates deeply. Just as I look up to iconic series you all know, I aspire for "Golden Mist" to be a source of inspiration. This first volume is not just a book; it's a vision I want to share with the world.

RedFManga

CHAPTER 01: "KAIZEN DAY

SO MASTER KAIZEN, AS THE NUMBER ONE HERO OF NOSHIBA AND OUR NEW SHOGUN, WHAT'S YOUR NEXT MOVE?
I'M GLAD YOU ASKED ANNOUNCER !!!
FOR YEARS, I'VE WANTED TWO THINGS!!
FIRST, TO BE THE SYMBOL OF PEACE FOR NOSHIBA AND ITS PEOPLE-!
POOF
AND SECOND, FOR EVERYONE TO LEARN AND ACKNOWLEDGE THE NEW ERA OF SCROLLS!
SO WITH MY OWN, I'LL MAKE SURE THAT DREAM IS REALIZED !!!

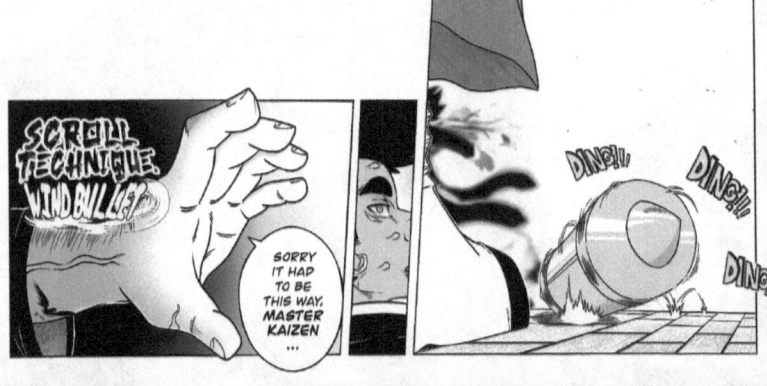

SCROLL TECHNIQUE. WIND BULLET!

SORRY IT HAD TO BE THIS WAY, MASTER KAIZEN...

DING!!!

DING!!!

DING!!!

DON'T LOOK AT ME LIKE THAT, I JUST WANTED TO SET AN EXAMPLE FOR THE PEOPLE WATCHING~!

THAT THIS SO-CALLED "AGE OF SCROLLS" ENDS NOW!

DAMMIT! THIS SCENARIO IS JUST LIKE ALL THE OTHERS.

IT'S LIKE PREVENTING KAIZEN'S DEATH SEEMS ALMOST IMPOSSIBLE NOW...

FWOOO!

...WILL THIS EVER END?

I'VE SEEN MILLIONS OF DIFFERENT SCENARIOS OF THIS MOMENT, SO WHY CAN'T I SEE A CLEAR-CUT FUTURE~?

FSHHH

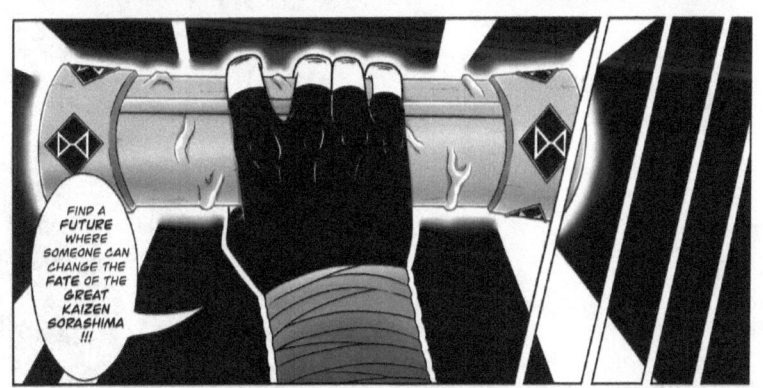

C'MON! FOCUS, KAI!

I'M TRYING!!!

KARATE CHOP!

BUMP

JUST A FEW MORE PALM STRIKES TO GO KID!

Beep! Beep! Beep!

TIME'S UP. CLASS IS OVER...

(SIGH) GUESS HE CAN'T TAKE A JOKE...

MASTER JIN
MASTER TO KAI

GEEZ, KAI'S SUPER EXHAUSTING...

BUT HE DOESN'T KNOW HOW RIGHT HE IS.

BELLA, DID YOU EVER GET THE CHANCE TO TELL HIM THAT THE DOJO'S CLOSING DOWN SOON?

WAIT, WHY WOULD I TELL HIM!? DO IT YOURSELF!

COME ON, I DON'T WANNA BE THE BEARER OF BAD NEWS... BESIDES, YOU TWO HAVE BEEN FRIENDS FOR A LONG TIME. IT'S BETTER IF YOU DO IT THAN ME.

MAN, WHY IS **MASTER JIN** SO SENSITIVE LATELY?!

I DON'T KNOW DAD. HE'S ALREADY BEEN THROUGH A LOT....

ESPECIALLY AFTER THE FIRE INCIDENT WITH HIS **GRANDPA** A YEAR AGO...

I'VE NEVER SEEN ANYONE LOOK THE WAY **KAI** DID THAT NIGHT... IT WAS LIKE HE WAS BROKEN, UNTIL...

IT ALL CHANGED AFTER HE MET US AND JOINED "KARATE CHOP".

. SO THIS IS YOUR GRANDPA'S DOJO HUH?

FWO.

I'M SORRY FOR YOUR LOSS... I KNOW IT'S HARD TO LOSE PEOPLE YOU CARE ABOUT...

IF YOU WANNA PLACE TO CRASH, COME TO MY DADS DOJO! ALSO, THE NAME'S **BELLA!**

KAI...

TPI

IF I TELL HIM THAT THE DOJO'S CLOSING DOWN, HE'LL BE THE SAME WAY HE WAS BACK THEN, ALONE!

WELL, MAYBE THAT'S A GOOD THING. AND BESIDES, I'M HAPPY THAT OLD MAN'S GONE... ALL HE DID WAS BRAINWASH **KAI** INTO THINKING HE'S SPECIAL—

JUST BECAUSE **MASTER KAIZEN** WAS THE SYMBOL OF PEACE.

~PNEF

WELL, THOSE TIMES HAVE PASSED, EVERYONE'S **FORGOTTEN** HIM..

THIS **DOJO** MIGHT BE INSPIRED BY **MASTER KAIZEN**, BUT HE'S A NOBODY OUTSIDE THESE DOORS... I JUST WISH **KAI** KNEW THAT.

WHAT IF I GIVE YOU A DAY OFF TOMORROW?

ANYWAY, HE TRUSTS YOU MORE THAN ANYONE ELSE RIGHT NOW.

I'LL **PASS.**

HEYYY KAI!!

BELLA? WHAT ARE YOU DOING HERE?

DON'T TELL ME. **MASTER JIN** BROUGHT YOU HERE TO TALK TO ME?

I'M OFFENDED! TWO BUDDIES CAN'T TALK CASUALLY NOWADAYS?

LEADING THE WHOLE CLAN TO BE LOST IN TIME, AS WELL AS KAIZEN'S DREAM.

(sigh)
...

HEH, YOU KNOW YOU MENTION THIS FACT LIKE EVERY WEEK, RIGHT?

BARELY ANYONE EVEN KNOWS WHO THE GOLDEN MIST ARE, AND THE PEOPLE THAT KNOW KAIZEN THINK HIS LEGACY WAS MEANT TO BE FORGOTTEN...

YEAH, BUT I CAN'T HELP IT! THEY WERE ALL BIG PARTS OF MY FAMILY'S HISTORY, NOT TO MENTION NOSHIBA.

WITHOUT THEM, THIS PLACE WOULD'VE NEVER EVEN EXISTED TO US...

BUT I THINK THEY'RE WRONG...

ONE DAY, I'LL BE STRONG ENOUGH TO MAKE EVERYONE KNOW WHAT KAIZEN'S DREAM REALLY MEANS!

FOR GRANDPA'S SAKE...

FWOO!

I'LL MAKE THIS QUICK!

WHAT THE HELL IS THAT!?

BELLA?!

BELLA, YOU SEE THIS!?

SH

In this zone, time is in my hands..

Not just her, but everything around us is frozen in time.

HUH? I COULD'VE SWORN I WAS JUST FIGHTING WITH THAT **CLOAKED GUY** A SECOND AGO...

WAIT... WHERE DID THESE PEOPLE COME FROM?

THE PATH I WAS JUST ON NEVER HAD AS MUCH OF A CROWD AS THIS.

WHAT'S GOING ON?!

HEY, MOVE OUT OF THE WAY!

WHAT GUY STANDS IN THE MIDDLE OF **NOSHIBA**!

OH, SORRY... WAIT, DID YOU JUST SAY~?

NOSHIBA?!

FWOOO

HE'S GONE...

AND AFTER ALL THAT, I STILL DON'T KNOW WHAT'S GOING ON.

ssssss!!

金

ALSO KAIZEN'S DREAM, AND THAT FUTURE NONSENSE... WHAT WAS HE EVEN TALKING ABOUT?

HOW DOES HE EXPECT ME TO CHANGE NOSHIBA'S FUTURE IF I DON'T KNOW WHERE I AM? ESPECIALLY NOW THAT...

I'M... ALONE AGAIN.

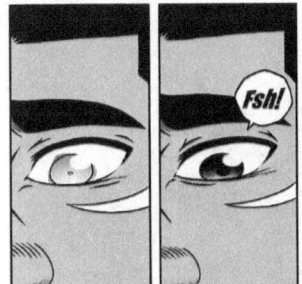

Fsh!

AND AFTER EVERYTHING I TOLD BELLA.

I'M STILL THE SAME GUY I WAS-

A YEAR AGO...

?

RUMBLE! RUMBLE! RUMBLE! RUMBLE! RUMBLE! RUMBLE!

?!

BOOM!

W-WHAT THE HELL WAS THAT ?!

DID I JUST GET HIT BY A GIANT FIST?!

AND I THOUGHT THINGS COULDN'T GET ANY WORSE..

?!

HEY, PIG? DON'T THINK YOU CAN GET AWAY FROM ME SO EASILY!

TP!

RAIDEN, THAT'S ENOUGH. WE AGREED TO CATCH HIM, NOT HURT HIM!

Golden Mist!

ICHI TAMASHI

VICE CAPTAIN OF THE GOLDEN MIST

HINA ORITSU

GOLDEN MIST 5TH YEAR

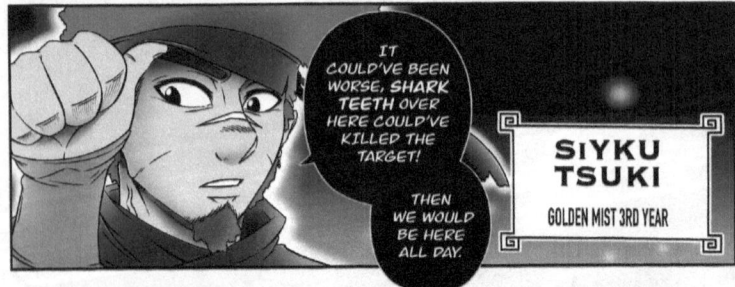

SIYKU TSUKI

GOLDEN MIST 3RD YEAR

YIRI MITSUKO

GOLDEN MIST 10TH YEAR

SO WE'RE JUST GOING TO IGNORE WHAT SIYKU SAID?!

FINE! KEEP THAT ENERGY BECAUSE AFTER THIS, I'M GONNA MAKE YOU INTO A SHARK BUFFET!

RAIDEN MICHIRO

GOLDEN MIST 4TH YEAR

I HAVE SO MANY QUESTIONS, BUT I KNOW ONE THING FOR SURE—

I REALLY AM IN THE PAST...!

THIS IS UNREAL! MY **GRANDPA** TOLD ME SO MANY STORIES ABOUT EVERY SINGLE ONE OF YOU!

Thump!

ENOUGH MUMBLING!!!

I TOLD **RAIDEN** TO CATCH YOU FOR A REASON, AND IT'S TO ASK—

WHY THE HELL, DO YOU HAVE **KAIZEN'S** AURA?

KAIZEN'S AURA? I- I DON'T EVEN KNOW WHAT THAT MEANS. ALSO, WHY THE ATTACK?!

YOU GUYS ARE SUPPOSED TO PROTECT CITIZENS IN NOSHIBA... R-RIGHT?

PROTECTING THEM FROM YOU.

DA-DOOM

THAT'S ACTUALLY WHAT WE'RE DOING.

NOT ONE PERSON HAS THE SAME AURA AS KAIZEN, BUT YOU DO.

ALSO, BY THE LOOKS OF YOUR CLOTHES, YOU SEEM LIKE YOU'RE NOT EVEN FROM NOSHIBA TO BEGIN WITH!

DO YOU THINK...?

I DO.

CRAP! HE CAUGHT THAT, THIS IS BECOMING A BIG MISUNDERSTAND-ING...

YOUNG MAN, YOU'RE COMING WITH US FOR FURTHER QUESTIONING–

FOR BEING A POSSIBLE MEMBER OF THE **HIDDEN CROW CLAN!**

HIDDEN CROW...? THE HELL'S THAT?

YOU CAN ACT IN DENIAL ALL YOU WANT, BUT IT ISN'T CHANGING YOUR OUTCOME!

SCREW IT, I HAVE TO TELL THEM EVERYTHING! MAYBE, THEY'LL HELP ME GET BACK HOME!

TCH!

ALRIGHT!!

AS CRAZY AS THIS MIGHT SOUND, MY NAME IS **KAI SORASHIMA** THE DESCENDENT OF MASTER **KAIZEN!!**

AND I WAS SENT HERE FROM THE **FUTURE** BY CLOAKED GUY NAMED JI–

W-WHY IS THIS HAPPENING ?!

WRONG MOVE!!

MY WHOLE LIFE...

GRANDPA TOLD ME THAT THE GOLDEN MIST WOULD NEVER HURT THE INNOCENT, BUT-

THEY'VE ALREADY CLASSIFIED ME AS AN-

ENEMY...

I CAN'T BELIEVE IT!

H-HE ACTUALLY HIT RAIDEN!

SKRRRRR

THD!

FWO!

HUF

HUF

HUF

YOU MADE IT SOUND LIKE YOU KNEW EVERYTHING ABOUT ME!

SWOOOO

BUT IN THE END..

WHAT YOU JUST SAID...

I MIGHT NOT BE **SPECIAL**, BUT AT LEAST I DON'T BRING DOWN THE NAMES THAT ARE...

DOMF!

Fwoo!

EVEN SO...

SOMEHOW, A SMALL PART OF ME ACTUALLY HOPED YOU WERE TELLING THE TRUTH ABOUT ALL THE **KAIZEN** STUFF..

BUT I SEE, I WAS WRONG IN THE END...

I GET IT NOW...

I GUESS I NEVER REALLY KNEW **KAIZEN'S** REAL **DREAM** AFTERALL...

SO EVEN IF YOU DON'T SEE HIM, YOUR GRANDPA WILL ALWAYS BE WITH YOU.

AND FROM NOW ON... SO WILL I.

SO I'M GONNA ASK AGAIN.

ARE YOU COMING?

I MIGHT NOT BE BACK IN MY TIME, BUT THAT DOESN'T MEAN I'M ALONE!!!

THOUGH THEY'RE NOT HERE...

BELLA!

JIN!

AND EVEN...

GRANDPA...

I GUESS MY SCROLL WAS RIGHT. I UNDERESTIMATED THIS KID!

THANKS TO HIM, IT LOOKS LIKE WE HAVE A FIGHTING CHANCE!

BUT THIS FIGHT'S NOT OVER YET! IT'S ONLY JUST BEGUN!

SO SHOW ME, GREAT DESCENDANT !!!

SHOW ME THE POWER YOU HAVE! NOT JUST TO SAVE NOSHIBA'S FUTURE~!

BUT TO END CURSE!!!

FWOO

OSH!

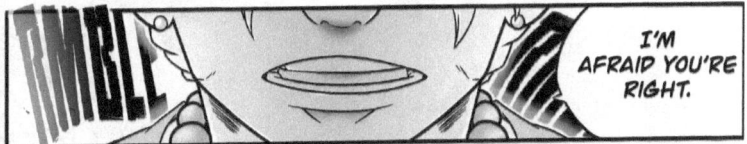

NO, NO, NO! WHY DID YOU USE YOUR TECHNIQUE? I TOLD YOU ALL NOT TO INTERFERE!

DOMF!

DON'T ACT STUPID. IF YOU KEPT GOING, YOU WOULD'VE KILLED HIM!

HIS BODY WAS ALREADY PAST ITS LIMIT...

?

SAME GOES FOR THE CIVILIANS YOU WERE TRYING TO PROTECT, AS WELL...

O-OH SORRY.

I GUESS I OVERDID IT AGAIN...

IT'S OKAY. JUST HELP ME GET THIS KID OUT OF HERE.

NO WAY!

HE'S EXTREMELY DANGEROUS! RAIDEN WAS RIGHT. THE SERVANTS CAN HANDLE HIM.

BESIDES, LET'S NOT FORGET ABOUT OUR URGENT MISSION!

SUCH AN AMAZING FIGHT!!

AT FIRST, I DIDN'T SEE IT BUT–

I DO NOW ...

WHEN I MET THAT KID, I SAW NO POTENTIAL IN HIM, BUT NOW I KNOW EVERY FLOWER BLOOMS WITHIN IT'S OWN TIME.

I KNOW YOU FELT THAT KAIZEN... BECAUSE THAT'S–

SIR, THE CEREMONY'S BEGINNING SHORTLY, SO BE READY!

READY? HOW COULD I NOT BE ?!

IT'S A BIG DAY AFTER ALL!

THE POWER THAT WILL CHANGE YOUR FATE!

CHAPTER 02: "KAIZEN'S DREAM" PART 1

N-NO PLEASE.. S-SPARE ME!!
?!
DOMF!
I BEG YOU! I DID NOTHING WRO-
AGAIN, I APOLOGIZE ...MASTER KAIZEN
HUH ?
BUT THIS IS THE FATE THAT NOSHIBA MUST FACE...

WAIT! MASTER TENOHIRA!!

HOW LONG ARE WE SUPPOSED TO KEEP HIM IN HERE?

I HAVE NO IDEA, MAYBE UNTIL EMPEROR SAYS SO?

MAN, SHE REALLY EXPECTS US TO CONTAIN THE STRONGEST WARRIOR IN NOSHIBA?

FWOO

YEP, WE'RE FIRED...

GOLDEN MIST ROYAL PALACE:

MAIN ROOM

UM.. MASTER?

THE FLOORS ARE CLEAN, THE WALLS ARE SCRUBBED, AND THE DECORATIONS ARE BEING SET, SO FAR SO GOOD.

MASTER, I NEED TO HAVE A WORD WITH YOU!

MASTER TENOHIRA

KAIZEN'S TEACHER/ LEADER

EVERYONE'S JOB IS TO CLEAN THE PALACE RIGHT NOW! SO WHY AREN'T YOU DOING THAT!?

OH M-MY APOLOGIES!

TP!
TP!
TP!
TP!
TP!

THE THING IS I WAS GONNA LET YOU KNOW THAT—

WAIT, YOU MEAN A CEREMONY ?!

THAT'S CORRECT! IT DOESN'T START TILL NOON BUT—

PLEASE BEHAVE APPROPRIATELY TILL THEN KAIZEN.

KAIZEN ?...

THAT'S WEIRD! THAT DREAM WAS ABOUT MY CEREMONY TOO!

C-COULD THIS BE A COINCIDENCE ?!

?!

SNAP!!

THERE YOU GO IGNORING ME AGAIN! WHAT'S UP WITH YOU!?

I THOUGHT YOU WOULD BE MORE EXCITED, BUT I GUESS I SHOULD CHOOSE SOMEONE ELSE!
I-IT'S NOTHING MASTER, I WAS JUST SURPRISED THAT'S ALL!
H-HEY YOU GUYS?
WELL I'M GLAD THEN...
I STILL WISH YOU STAYED IN YOUR ROOM THOUGH, COULD'VE SURPRISED YOU WITH ANOTHER GIFT BUT YOU'RE STUBBORN.
THIS IS AN HONOR, I WON'T LET YOU DOWN!
YEAH, SORRY ABOUT THAT TOO!
I WANT TO TELL MASTER TENOHIRA ABOUT MY DREAM BUT SHE'LL PROBABLY JUST THINK I'M CRAZY...
AND TO BE HONEST I COULD BE OVERTHINKING IT MYSELF.
IT'S JUST... WHY DO I HAVE A GUT FEELING SOMETHING'S OFF?..

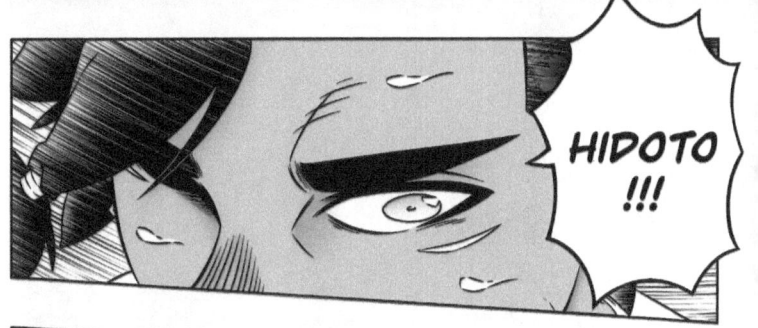

HIDOTO
!!!

BADUM7

GRIP!

BADUM7

EVERY
-ONE
RUN!!

BADUM7

BADUM7

SCROLL
TECHNIQUE.

SUPRESSION

NOT THIS AGAIN !!

FWSH!

WHAT HAS GOTTEN INTO YOU TODAY?!

YOU KNOW SCROLL TECHNIQUES ARE NOT ALLOWED IN THE MAIN ROOM!! ESPECIALLY YOURS!

NOW THAT I HAVE YOUR ATTENTION, I HAVE SOME **IMPORTANT NEWS!**

I FOUND AN **URGENT SCROLL** IN FRONT OF THE PALACE EARLIER THIS MORNING!

THIS MORNING? LET ME SEE!

HUH ?!

BMP!

THE HIDDEN **CROWS** ARE TAKING OVER A **VILLAGE** NOT TO FAR FROM **NOSHIBA?**

IT'S ONE OF OUR **ALLIES** TOO!!

THE FACT THAT THE **HIDDEN CROW CLAN** IS UP TO THIS MAKES MY BLOOD BOIL!

EMPEROR, IF ANYONE OUTSIDE THIS **PALACE** KNOWS THAT A **VILLAGE** NEAR US IS GETTING TAKIN OVER, EVERYTHING IN **NOSHIBA** WOULD GO INTO CHAOS!!

YOU'RE RIGHT, THE **GOLDEN MIST** ARE GONNA HAVE TO TAKE CARE OF THIS **MISSION!** THIS CAN'T BE KNOWN TO THE PEOPLE COMING FOR THE **CEREMONY!**

WHY DIDN'T I TELL MASTER **TENOHIRA** WHAT HAPPEN-ED IN MY **DREAM** EARLIER?..

IS IT THAT I COULDN'T BEAR THE FACT OF TELLING HER HOW SHE DIED?

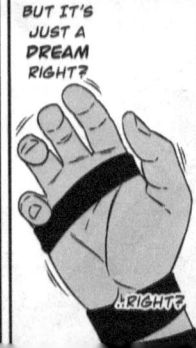

BUT IT'S JUST A **DREAM** RIGHT?

..RIGHT?

WAIT... WHAT IF IT WASN'T!
CLUTCH!!
IT WOULD MAKE SENSE.
HIDOTO'S PRESENCE THAT I NEVER FELT TILL NOW!!
THE CEREMONY!
AND FINALLY THE GOLDEN MIST LEAVING FOR A MISSION!
EVERY SITUATION THAT HAPPENED IN MY DREAM'S COMING TRUE!
COME ON ICHI!
...IT'S ALL MAKING SENSE NOW!!
THERE WAS NO DREAM !!
THAT WAS THE FUTURE!!

I WAS SOMEHOW SENT BACK IN **TIME** TO THE BEGINNING OF THE DAY!

BUT THERE'S ONLY ONE **PERSON** THAT COULD'VE DONE SOMETHING LIKE THIS—

AND HE SHOULD BE...!

MAN, KAIZEN!

CREEK!

?!

WHAT TYPE OF MESS DID YOU PUT **YOURSELF** INTO NOW ?!

EVERYONE!!

WHY ARE YOU IN THIS BOX SENSEI?

IS THIS TRAINING?

IT'S NOT A BOX, IT'S MASTER TENOHIRAS TECHNIQUE SO STOP TOUCHING IT!

MAN, FOR MASTER TO USE HER TECHNIQUE ON YOU, THIS MUST BE PRETTY SERIOUS!

DID YOU TWO HAVE A BATTLE ?!

PLEASE TELL ME HOW IT WENT?!

TAP TAP TAP TAP

WE ALL OVER-HEARD THE CONVERSA-TION!!

IT SOUNDS LIKE THE HIDDEN CROWS ARE TAKING OVER A VILLAGE! PROBABLY SOME LOW TIER MEMBERS!!

WE'LL JUST TAKE THEM OUT BEFORE THEY GET CLOSE TO NOSHIBA AND KAIZEN'S CEREMONY !!

I COULD'VE SWORN I WAS JUST **FIGHTING** WITH THAT **CLOAKED GUY** A SECOND AGO.

WAIT... WHERE DID THESE PEOPLE COME FROM?

THE PATH I WAS JUST ON NEVER HAD AS MUCH OF A **CROWD** AS THIS!

WHAT'S GOING ON ?!

CHAPTER 03: "KAIZEN'S DREAM" PART 2

WOW KAIZEN! WITH ALL DUE RESPECT, A-ARE YOU SURE ABOUT THIS?!

IT'S AN UNKNOWN OUTCOME IF THEY GO... COULD BE A TRAP.

YES, I AM...

BUT SIR, YOU'LL MISS THE CEREMONY, DON'T YOU CARE ABOUT BEING NOSHIBAS NEW SHOGUN?

IS IT BECAUSE OF MY AGE I'VE GOTTEN SO WEAK?!

SLAM

BESIDES... THE CEREMONY ISN'T THAT IMPORTANT TO ME ANYWAYS!

I CAN'T LOSE EVERYONE! NOT LIKE THAT...

I'M SORRY, BUT IT'S MY DECISION AS THE LEADER OF THIS TEAM!

HE'S RIGHT.. I UNDERESTIMATED MY TEAM.

... MAYBE IN THAT FUTURE THEY EVEN STOPPED HIDOTO FOR ME...

YOUR IMMATURITY WON'T BE TOLERATED ANY LONGER, GO GET READY-

SMACK!!

?!

BEFORE YOU CAUSE EVEN MORE TROUBLE FOR YOUR -SELF !!!

OK, OK GEEZ!

ALSO, WHATEVER YOU'RE GOING THROUGH WITH HIDOTO, GET IT RESOLVED SOONER RATHER THAN LATER!

I DON'T WANT THIS TO BE A PROBLEM DURING THE CEREMONY !!

FINE! BUT DID YOU REALLY HAVE TO SLAP ME JUST TO SAY THAT?!

SLAP!

SLAP!

SLAP!

SLAP!

EVERY-ONE GET BACK TO WORK!
WE DON'T HAVE ALL DAY!!
THAT GOT A LITTLE CRAZY EARLIER, DON'T YOU THINK EMPEROR TENOHIRA?
YOU'RE STILL FOLLOWING ME...?
W-WELL YEAH, I ACTUALLY WANTED TO ASK A QUESTION ABOUT THAT SITUATION!
YOU SEE, I'M NEW HERE BUT-
DAMMIT, WHY ARE YOU ACTING LIKE YOU DON'T KNOW WHAT YOU DID TO ME THEN!!
BY THE LOOKS OF IT, IT SEEMS LIKE KAIZEN'S HATED HIDOTO FOR A VERY LONG TIME.
I WANTED TO ASK IF IT'S ALWAYS BEEN THAT WAY?
TMP!
ACTUALLY NO...
CRAZY ENOUGH, I'VE NEVER SEEN KAIZEN ACT LIKE THAT TOWARDS HIDOTO BEFORE!

FINALLY! AFTER ALL THE SHENANIGANS TODAY, IT SEEMS WE'RE DONE SETTING UP FOR THE **CEREMONY!**

THANK GOODNESS!

RRRRRRR!

NOT QUITE! **EMPEROR,** SOME SERVANTS NEED HELP WITH THE **CONFETTI** OUTSIDE!

AND I'M GUARDING THE FRONT, SO MY HANDS ARE FULL!

NOT A PROBLEM, I KNOW JUST THE **SERVANT** THAT CAN—

HELP ...?

WAIT, WHERE'D THAT GLASSES GIRL GO?!

E-EXCUSE ME? AM I MISSING SOMETHING HERE?!

YEAH, THAT **SERVANT** WITH THE **SCROLL** EARLIER, JUST RANDOMLY DISAPPEARED ON ME!

HOLD ON, SOMEONE BROUGHT ONE IN THE **PALACE** ?!

THAT DOESN'T MAKE SENSE, I WAS OUTSIDE ALL MORNING AND I DIDN'T SEE ANYONE COME IN WITH A **SCROLL!**

NO IDEA! I KEPT WATCH THE WHOLE TIME—

AND THE ONLY PEOPLE THAT PASSED THE FRONT GATES WERE SERVANTS!

SOMETHINGS NOT RIGHT WHERE IS KAIZEN?!

BOOM!

?!

THAT NOISE ...!

GUESS I WAS RIGHT THEN, HIDOTO WASN'T THE ONLY ONE!

YOU GAVE THE GOLDEN MIST THAT DISTRESS SCROLL EARLIER! I SHOULD'VE KNOWN YOU WERE THE MASTER MIND BEHIND ALL THAT!

GRRR!

WHAT DID YOU DO WITH MY TEAM?!

LET'S JUST SAY I LIED A LITTLE !!!

THAT SCROLL I GAVE THE GOLDEN MIST WASN'T WRITTEN BY A VILLAGE IN NEED OF SAVING~!

BUT INSTEAD, THOUSANDS OF HIDDEN CROW MEMBERS THAT ARE PLANNING ON AMBUSHING YOUR CLAN!

THAT ALLY VILLAGE BEING ATTACKED WASN'T REAL?...

SO IT WAS A TRAP!

CIRU

ASSASSIN FOR THE HIDDEN CROW CLAN...

OH, IT WAS, AND THE GOLDEN MIST ARE STRONG, BUT NO MATCH FOR MY MEN! THEY'RE PRACTICALLY LEADING THEMSELVES TO AN EARLY GRAVE AS WE SPEAK!!

HA! AND ALL THAT'S LEFT FOR ME TO DO IS KILL YOU AND CLAIM IT SUICIDE!

HA!

HA!

SCROLL TECHNIQUE: GOLDEN WAVE THIRD FORM!

SHUT UP!!

DASH!!

HUH? NOTHINGS HAPPEN-ING!

CMON KAIZEN I THOUGHT YOU WHERE SMARTER THEN THAT?

YOU KNOW MORE THAN ANYONE THAT YOU CAN'T USE A TECHNIQUE-!

WITHOUT A SCROLL CONNECTED TO YOU!

FWOOM!

FWOOM!

FWOOM!

FWOOM!

I TOOK YOURS DURING THE EXPLOSION EARLIER!!

BMF!

SO YOU COULDN'T AVOID THIS!...

SCROLL TECHNI

DEMON FEATHER BARRAGE

YOU MET YOUR MATCH, KAIZEN SORASHIMA!!!

WHAT A SHAME ...

THIS WHOLE TIME I COULD NEVER SEE WHY *TENOHIRA* CHOSE YOU TO BE NOSHIBA'S NEW SHOGUN ...

THERE'S LITERALLY NOTHING SPECIAL ABOUT YOU OTHER THEN YOUR *SCROLL*... WHAT A DISAPPOINT-MENT!

ZWISH

S-SCREW YOU!...

OH! NOT DEAD I SEE?!

TALK ALL YOU WANT... BUT AT LEAST I'M NO TRAITOR!

YOU LIED TO KILL THE GOLDEN MIST ....THEN YOU DECEIVED MASTER TENOHIRA JUST TO KILL ME!

HOW SAD... YOU MUST REALLY BE OBSESSED!

LIKE I'D CARE FOR SCUM LIKE YOU!!

!....

KRAK AK

KR

KRAK

KRAK

THE ONLY REASON WHY I DID ALL THIS WAS BECAUSE MY HIGHER UPS WANTED ME TO TAKE YOUR SCROLL!
KRAK
KRAK
SO AFTER I KILL YOU, THAT'S EXACTLY WHAT I'LL DO!
KRAK
SO DIE ALREADY !!!
KRAK
KRAK
KRAK
STMP!
WAIT WHAT?! I WAS JUST ABOUT TO KILL HIM, WHERE'D HE GO?
AND WHAT THE HECK'S UP WITH THE GROUND?! IT'S LIKE IT'S COMPLETELY INTACT-!
HFF
HFF
HFF

CHAPTER 04: "KAIZEN'S DREAM" PART 3

A PERSON CAN ONLY USE A TECHNIQUE OR CAN EMIT THEIR AURA WHEN THEY HAVE A SCROLL DIRECTLY ATTACHED TO THEM.
SCROLL TECHNIQUE.
BUT SOMEHOW, THIS KAIZEN LOOK ALIKE DOESN'T SEEM TO NEED ONE!
IS THIS TRULY THE POWER OF THE SORASHIMAS ?!
FSHH
FSHH
FSHH

NO HUMAN HAS BEEN ABLE TO MANIFEST THEIR AURA BY THEMSELVES SINCE THE ERA OF SCRIPTURES!

SO HOW ARE YOU DOING IT?

GUESS YOUR HIGHER UPS DIDN'T TELL YOU ENOUGH ABOUT ME. HUH?

FSHH

FSHH

FSHH

YOU SEE, IM NOT DOING THIS MYSELF!

I'M JUST MORE IN SYNC WITH MY SCROLL NOW, THAN EVER BEFORE!

FWOO

OSM!!

WITHOUT TOUCHING IT? THAT DOESN'T MAKE SENSE!

MIND IF I SHOW YOU EXACTLY WHAT THAT MEANS?!

FSHH

FSHH

FSHH

FSH...

FSHH

FSHH

NO NEED! I'LL JUST SEE FOR MYSELF!!

!!
NOW, LET'S SEE YOU ESCAPE THIS!!!
DEMON FEATHER BARRAGE
THIS ISN'T GOOD, I'M WAY PAST MY ORIGINAL PLAN, I NEED TO MAKE A NEW ONE!
BUT TO DO SO, I HAVE TO FIGURE OUT WHAT THAT ABILITY WAS EARLIER!
I WANNA SAY IT WAS SOME TYPE OF ILLUSION TECHNIQUE. HOWEVER, IT FELT LIKE MORE THAN THAT...
IF SO... HE WARNED ME ABOUT THIS!
YOU WANT ME TO SNEAK INTO NOSHIBA-!
AND PRETEND TO BE A SERVANT FOR THE GOLDEN MIST?!
PSH
I CRUSHED HIM, BUT THEN HE WAS INTACT!
PSH
PSH
PSH
COULD IT BE MY PERCEPTION OF REALITY WAS WARPED?!
PSH

INDEED.

ON THE DAY OF THE CEREMONY, I ALREADY SCHEDULED AN ARMY TO BE AT A SPECIFIC AREA.

ALL YOU NEED TO DO IS LEAD THE GOLDEN MIST THERE~!

SO YOU CAN FINISH OFF KAIZEN YOURSELF, AND TAKE HIS MOST POWERFUL WEAPON!

THE LEGEND-ARY SCROLL OF JIN-KOI!

WHAT?! THEY'RE ALL GOING BACK IN MY SCROLL!

IS THIS HOW IT WORKS ?!

SHOOO

WHEN MY **TECHNIQUE'S** ACTIVATED, MY AURA CREATES A VOID, WHERE I'M CAPABLE OF MANIPULATING THE COURSES OF YOUR ATTACKS!

PRETTY MUCH, YEAH!

FSHH

FSHH

FSHH

IN OTHER WORDS, THAT'S HOW I SURVIVED ALL YOUR TRICKS EARLIER!

SO YOU CAN PLAN AS MUCH AS YOU'D LIKE, CIRU.

TCH!

I SET YOUR **FATE** SINCE THE VERY BEGINNING.

FSHH

FSHH

YOU **LOST** WHEN YOU DIDN'T KILL ME THE FIRST TIME!

FSHH

LOST?! I DON'T CARE HOW POWERFUL YOUR ABILITY IS-!

YOU'RE NOT UNBEAT-ABLE!

GRRRR

WSH

!!

SHOOO!

FWSHH

?!

YOU'RE RIGHT ABOUT THAT!!

I'VE SEEN MYSELF DIE FROM A SIMPLE WIND BULLET!

BUT THE THING IS, WITH THIS TECH-NIQUE OF MINE-!

FSHH

FSHH

FSHH

N-NO WAY.

I-I CAN'T MOVE MY BODY!

SHOO!

FSHH

FSHH

FSHH

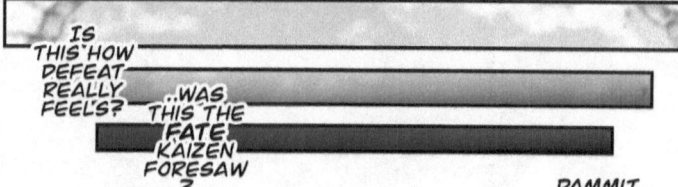

IS THIS HOW DEFEAT REALLY FEEL'S?

..WAS THIS THE FATE KAIZEN FORESAW?...

DAMMIT... HOW PATHETIC OF ME.

ALL I WANTED TO BE WAS MORE OF USE TO YOU—

MY LORD...

KAIZEN!!

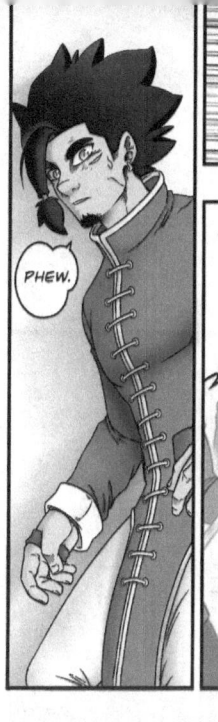

PHEW.

I GATHERED THE **SOLDIERS** AND CAME AS SOON A POSSIBLE!!

SHF

ARE YOU OK?!

MASTER TENOHIRA ?!

OH THANK GOODNESS, YOU ALREADY TOOK DOWN THE TRAITOR!

FOR A SECOND I WAS WORRIED!

GLAD YOU HAD THINGS HANDLED HERE!

141

YEAH... THANKS.

SHE WAS DEFINITELY A TOUGH ONE. AND THAT'S NOT EVEN MENTIONING HER **SCROLL.**

IF SHE WASN'T AN **ASSASSIN,** MAYBE HER SKILLS WOULD'VE BEEN A GREAT USE HERE...

DON'T GIVE SYMPATHY TO **HER!** SHE SHOULD BE PUNISHED EXTREMELY FOR DECEIVING US.

THANK YOU **KAIZEN,** I'LL TAKE IT FROM HERE.

GUARDS?!

HOLD ON!!!

SHOO

BEFORE YOU DO ANYTHING, THERE'S STILL ONE THING I WANT YOU TO SEE.

HUH?!

REMEMBER WHEN YOU TOLD ME TO **RESOLVE** THINGS EARLIER? WELL, IN THE END I COULDN'T DO IT...

AND I'M SORRY FOR THAT.

BUT NOW I CAN AT LEAST SHOW YOU WHY.

. . .

ON HER ARM, IS THE MARKING FOR THE HIDDEN CROWS-

WHICH EVERYONE IN THEIR CLAN HAS, INCLUDING HIDOTO!

DA-DOON

FWOOO

THE REAL REASON CIRU ATTACKED ME WAS BECAUSE-

SHE DIDN'T WANT ME SPREADING THAT INFORM-ATION.

SO SHE WAS HIRED?

AND YOU HAVE PROOF THIS TIME?

I JUST NEED YOUR HELP TO PROVE IT.

I DO.

STEP STEP STEP STEP STEP STEP

DMF

I HEARD KAIZEN WAS UP HERE!

HUF HUF

WHERE IS HE ?!

HUF

WHAT'S THIS?! WHY IS EVERYONE JUST STANDING HERE?

IS IT TRUE? WAS HE INJURED DURING THAT EXPLOSION ?!

HE'S NOT THE ONE YOU SHOULD BE CONCERNED ABOUT, HIDOTO.

SUPRESSION

?!

HEY! WHAT'S THE MEANING OF THIS?!

ENOUGH WITH THE ACT!

YOUR FRIEND'S BEEN CAUGHT, AND ALL THAT'S LEFT IS YOU!

IT'S FINALLY TIME YOU GOT WHAT YOU DESERVE. NOW—!

HOLD STILL.

?!

SO KAIZEN WAS RIGHT ALL ALONG. YOU'RE A HIDDEN CROW!

DA— —DOON

HOW COULD YOU BETRAY US LIKE THIS? I TRUSTED YOU!

HE KNOWS ABOUT THE MARK?

KNOW WHAT? DON'T ANSWER—!

CAUSE YOU'RE DONE.

W-WAIT, MY SCROLL!!!

Shh

I'VE BEEN FOOLED FOR TOO LONG.

GUARDS! BRING HIDOTO AND HIS ACCOMPLICE TO THE PRISON ROOM AND KEEP THEM THERE!

UWOO!

HOLD ON, THIS IS A BIG MISUNDER-STANDING! I HELPED RAISE KAIZEN!

HE IS LIKE A SON TO ME... I WOULD NEVER BETRAY HIM!

ZMMM

I MIGHT ONLY BE YOUR SERVANT—

BUT, YOU'RE LIKE A SON TO ME, KAIZEN.

I DON'T KNOW WHAT WAS IN YOUR HEAD FOR ALL THOSE YEARS. BUT, YOU WERE JUST A SERVANT!

NOTHING MORE NOTHING LESS!

SIR.

SORRY I DIDN'T BELIEVE YOU AT FIRST... THE EVIDENCE WAS RIGHT IN FRONT OF ME.

IT'S FINE, MASTER—

NO IT'S NOT!

YOU TRUSTED YOUR INTUITION EVEN WHEN NO ONE ELSE AGREED WITH YOU, EVEN ME.

I'M PROUD OF YOU KAIZEN. ONCE AGAIN, YOU HAVE SHOWN WHY I'VE CHOSEN YOU AS OUR SHOGUN.

HAVE I REALLY?... IT WAS ME THAT LET THE GOLDEN MIST GO ON THAT MISSION—

EVEN WHEN I KNEW IT WAS A TRAP.

HOW COULD I EVER CALL MYSELF THAT IF I CAN'T EVEN BE A LEADER?

THE GOLDEN MIST DIDN'T LEAVE NOSHIBA!

WHY... WHY WOULD YOU TELL ME THIS?!

LIKE I SAID, YOU'RE LIKE A SON TO ME...

THAT TRAITOR HAS THE AUDACITY TO SAY THAT AGAIN?!

LIKE WE'D BELIEVE THAT...

• • •

ACTUALLY...

OUT OF EVERY-THING... I THINK THAT ONE WAS THE TRUTH.

FSHH FSHH FSHH FSHH

FWAH

THE BATTLE FOR THE FUTURE IS FINALLY OVER... AT LEAST FOR NOW.

OH... I SEE.

AND YET, I FEEL LIKE THERE'S STILL MORE QUESTIONS THAN ANSWERS.

WHAT WAS THE **HIDDEN CROWS** REAL PLAN?

WHERE DID THAT UNUSUAL AMOUNT OF **AURA** COME FROM-?

IN THE MIDST OF THE **FIGHT**?

AND FINALLY, HOW WAS I ABLE TO REMEMBER A SEPARATE TIMELINE?

THESE ANSWERS MIGHT BE FEW AND FAR BETWEEN, BUT I WILL SOLVE THEM ALL...

AND WHEN I DO... THAT'S WHEN I'LL TRULY ACCEPT MYSELF AS A SHOGUN.

SIR THE CEREMONY'S BEGINNING SHORTLY, SO BE READY!

READY? HOW COULD I NOT BE?

IT'S A BIG DAY AFTER ALL!

I SEE MASTER KAIZEN'S BACK TO NORMAL.

GUYS, LOOK OUTSIDE!!!

?!

FOR NOW HOWEVER...

I'LL JUST REMEMBER WHAT ICHI TOLD ME.

TO DO MY PART...

KNOCK

KNOCK

KNOCK

KNOCK

HOLD ON SIR! SOME GUARDS SPOTTED THE GOLDEN MIST!

SWSH

HUH?!

—AND THEY'RE CARRYING SOMEONE THAT LOOKS LIKE YOU!!

AND THE **GOLDEN MIST** WILL DO THEIRS.

CHAPTER 05: UNFORESEEN FUTURE

HUH?

WAS SCREAMING REALLY NECESSARY?...

MUST BE A FUTURE THING!

OR MAYBE IT WAS A NIGHTMARE, RAIDEN.

SKRATCH

GUYS, HE STILL RECOVERING FROM THE PREVIOUS BATTLE!

GO EASY ON HIM.

?....

WOW, S-STEP BACK YOU PSYCHOS!

PSH

OO

WOW!! YOU KNOW YOUR STUFF!

WELL SINCE YOU SEEM TO KNOW A LOT, THERE'S NO REASON FOR ME TO HIDE ANYTHING FROM YOU.

KAIZEN'S CEREMONY IS STARTING AND WE NEEDED A PLACE TO KEEP YOU UNTIL WE FIGURE OUT WHO YOU ARE.

YIRI, OUR STORIES HAVE BEEN TOLD ACROSS THE COUNTRY.

WHAT? DIDN'T I ALREADY TELL YOU I WAS FROM THE FUTURE?

IT'S KIND OF SELF-EXPLANA-TORY!

WE'RE NOT RULING ANYTHING OUT YET.

WELL I AM!

LOOK, THIS FUTURE NONSENSE BETTER LEAVE YOUR MOUTH WHEN KAIZEN GETS HERE!

BECAUSE YOU MIGHT BE ABLE TO TRICK RAIDEN, BUT NOT US.

NOW INFORM EVERYONE ON HOW YOUR AURA LOOKS IDENTICAL TO KAIZEN'S JIN-KOI SCROLL?

J~JIN WHAT?!

BY ANY CHANCE, ARE YOU WORKING WITH THE HIDDEN CROWS?

CAN YOU MIMIC PEOPLES ABILITIES?

HOW MANY TIMES HAVE I BEATEN SIYKU IN A DUEL? SPOIL ME!

WHAT IS THIS, 21 QUESTIONS?!

HOW AM I SUPPOSED TO ANSWER ALL THAT ~?

WAIT, DID YOU SAY KAIZEN WAS COMING?

BUT UNFORT-UNATELY... WE DIDN'T TRAVEL ANYWHERE!

HUH?!!

YEAH, WE GOT SIDE TRACK-ED IN NOSHIBA!

AND HOW'D THAT HAPPEN?!

GUESS I WAS RIGHT TO BELIEVE HIDOTO AFTER ALL.

I'LL MAKE IT QUICK! FIRST, WE ENCOUNT-ERED THIS STRANGE GUY ON OUR PATH~!

WHICH SURPRISINGLY ENOUGH, HAS A LOT OF SIMILARITIES TO YOU!

I'VE HEARD.

SO I BROUGHT HIM HERE FOR YOU TO TALK TO!

WAIT, WHY ME?

THE GOLDEN MIST AND I STILL HAVE THAT MISSION TO COMPLETE, SO WE'RE KIND OF SHORT ON TIME YA KNOW~!

ACTUALLY, THAT'S WHAT I WANTED TO TALK TO YOU ABOUT!

A LOT HAS CAME TO LIGHT ABOUT THIS SO CALLED MISSION.

AND YOU NEED TO HEAR ABOUT IT...

WHY WON'T YOU LISTEN TO ME?! I'VE SAID IT A MILLION TIMES, I'M FROM THE FUTURE!
DON
ENOUGH WITH YOUR LIES! YOU CAN ROT IN THERE UNTIL KAIZEN COMES!
GEEZ! THEY ACCEPT PEOPLE WITH LIZARD ARMS BUT NOT TIME TRAVEL?!
THIS ERA IS SO BACK-WARDS!
WELL ON THE BRIGHT SIDE, I'LL FINALLY GET TO MEET MY GREAT ANCESTOR RIGHT?
IF MY WHOLE BODY WASN'T IN PAIN, I WOULD PROBABLY SAY THIS IS A DREAM COME TRUE!

HEY I THINK THIS IS YOURS CHUBBY!

HUH? THIS IS MY JACKET BUT HOW?!

SIYKU USED HIS SHADOW WARPING WHATEVER TO GRAB IT FROM THE VILLAGE.

UNLESS YOU'RE TELLING ME HOW MANY VICTORIES I'VE HAD IN THE FUTURE—

I DON'T NEED TO HEAR A SINGLE WORD FROM YOU..

NOW CAN YOU STOP TALKING TO YOUR-SELF-?!

DOOM!

...I'M HAPPY AT LEAST SOMEONE BELIEVES ME.

FWOOO...

SO THAT CIRU CHICK REALLY WAS BEHIND ALL THIS, HUH?

TP

TP

YEAH, AND SHE WAS ALSO THE ONE THAT SENT THE DISTRESS SCROLL.

BUT I DIDN'T LISTEN...

Clutch!!

THIS IS MY FAULT... YOU TRIED TO STOP US EARLIER BY GOING ON YOUR OWN—

HEY, DON'T BLAME YOUR-SELF!

THE HIDDEN CROWS ARE JUST GETTING WAY MORE CALCULATED WITH THEIR ATTACKS.

...ALL THAT MATTERS IS THAT YOU GUYS ARE ALIVE.

YEAH...

I'M SORRY FOR **HIDOTO** BY THE WAY, I KNEW YOU TWO WERE CLOSE.

THANKS BUT, AT THE END OF THE DAY I HAD TO DO WHAT WAS BEST FOR THE VILLAGE-

SO IF YOU DON'T MIND ME ASKING, HOW DID YOU FIGURE HIM OUT?

JUST YESTERDAY YOU TWO WERE HANGING OUT LIKE ALWAYS.

BUT ALL OF A SUDDEN TODAY YOU CONVICT HIM OF BEING A **TRAITOR?**

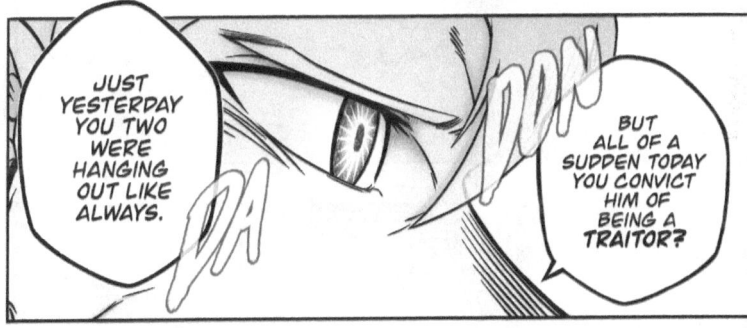

I THINK THERE'S MORE TO THE **STORY~!**

THAT YOU'RE NOT TELLING ME!

I DON'T KNOW WHAT YOU'RE TALKING ABOUT.

DON'T GIVE ME THAT **KAIZEN!** YOU KNOW MORE THAN ANYONE THAT THE **GOLDEN MIST** WAS CREATED BASED ON TRUST.

EVEN THOUGH YOUR BECOMING **SHOGUN,** THAT DOESN'T MEAN THAT RULE DOESN'T APPLY TO YOU ANYMORE!

NOW, TELL ME WHY YOU'VE BEEN ACTING SO DIFFERENT!

FINE! I THINK **JIKEN'S** STILL ALIVE SOMEHOW—

HAPPY ?!

BEFORE WAKING UP TODAY, I SAW MYSELF LOOKING DOWN AT A CROWD THAT WAS CHEER-ING MY NAME!

ONLY FOR THE NEXT MOMENT, THE PERSON I'VE TRUSTED FOR YEARS SHOOTS ME IN THE BACK!

WHEN THAT HAPPENED, I WOKE UP NOTICING THAT I WAS RELIVING THE SAME MOMENTS FROM MY DREAM!

UNTIL I REALIZED IT WASN'T ONE... I WAS SENT BACK IN TIME TO THE BEGINNING OF THE DAY!

I DON'T KNOW IF MY PREVIOUS CONSCIOUSNESS IS IN ANOTHER VERSION OF MYSELF OR IF THE **TIMELINES** REPEATED BUT—

I FEEL LIKE JIKEN'S THE REASON I WAS GIVEN THIS SECOND CHANCE—

AND I NEED TO FIGURE OUT WHY!

HEH, SO WE'RE FINALLY ON THE SAME PAGE NOW.

?!

HE COULD POSSIBLY HAVE THE ANSWERS YOU'RE LOOKING FOR. NOT ONLY THAT, BUT HE CLAIMS TO BE FROM THE FUTURE...!

THE PERSON WE FOUND IN NOSHIBA SAID JIKEN'S NAME AS WELL.

WHAT'S TAKING KAIZEN AND ICHI SO LONG TO GET HERE?!

THEY BETTER NOT HAVE FORGOTTEN ABOUT THE MISSION!

NEITHER OF THEM WOULD DO THAT, HINA.

I AM A LITTLE CONCERNED, THOUGH.

ONE OF OUR ALLY VILLAGES ARE BEING ATTACKED RIGHT NOW-!

DNK

A MISSION, WHAT ARE THEY ON ABOUT?

WE WERE GOING TO HELP OUT, BUT SOMEONE KEPT US HERE!

IT'S YOU... I'M TALKING ABOUT YOU!

MISSION... WHY DO I FEEL LIKE I'M FORGETTING SOMETHING AGAIN.

I REPEAT, DON'T LEAVE!

WHEN I TOLD YOU GUYS THAT I WAS FROM THE FUTURE!

I WASN'T LYING!!

NOT THIS AGAIN.

UNTIL TODAY, I NEVER HEARD OF A JIN-KOI SCROLL!

SAME GOES FOR THIS HIDDEN CROW CLAN!

AND I DON'T UNDERSTAND EVERYONE'S OBSESSION WITH MY AURA!

BUT WHAT I DO KNOW, IS THAT I'M KAIZEN'S GREAT DESCEND-ANT!

SO PLEASE TRUST IN WHEN I'M ABOUT TO SAY!

TRUST YOU?! YOU'RE ACTING LIKE YOU'RE NOT THE ONE IN A CAGE RIGHT NOW!

I JUST RE-MEMBERED SOMETHING CRUCIAL TO YOUR SURVIVAL!!

FWSH

IN THE FUTURE, MY *GRANDPA* AND I HAVE BEEN TRYING TO FIND ANSWERS ABOUT WHAT HAPPENED TO YOU ALL FOR YEARS!

BECAUSE THE ONLY THING WE KNEW WAS THAT YOU ALL DIED DURING A *MYSTERIOUS MISSION*-!

ON THE DAY OF THE CEREMONY... SAME GOES FOR *KAIZEN!*

OBVIOUSLY, I DON'T KNOW WHAT'S GOING ON BEHIND THE SCENES, BUT YOU GUYS CAN'T LEAVE!
RAIDEN, YOU HAVE TO CONVINCE THEM TO TRUST ME!
THIS IS WHAT JIKEN MEANT BY CHANGING THE FUTURE!
HOW DARE YOU?!
UNLIKE EVERY -ONE, I BELIEVED YOU!
BUT THE FIRST THING YOU TELL US IS HOW WE ALL DIE?!
W-WAIT!
DOOON!
WHAT TYPE OF FOOL DO YOU TAKE ME FOR?!
GUAR

GRP
DOOM!!
DAMMIT, I CAN'T MOVE!
HE'S GOT ME GOOD!
SAY GOOD-NIGHT, PIG!!
FWMP
I'M DONE WITH YOUR LIES!!!
I DON'T THINK I CAN GET OUT OF THIS ONE!!
I WASN'T EVEN ABLE...
TO SEE. KAIZEN...
...SORRY GRAMPA.

IN THE NEXT VOLUME...

Kai and Kaizen's fateful encounter marks a significant turning point. However, unbeknownst to them, a lingering threat lies in the shadows as the ceremony looms ever closer. Will the imminent arrival of Kai herald a transformative shift in the timeline, altering the course of Kaizen's fate? Stay tuned as the Hidden Crows unveil their final hand, for the battle is far from over.

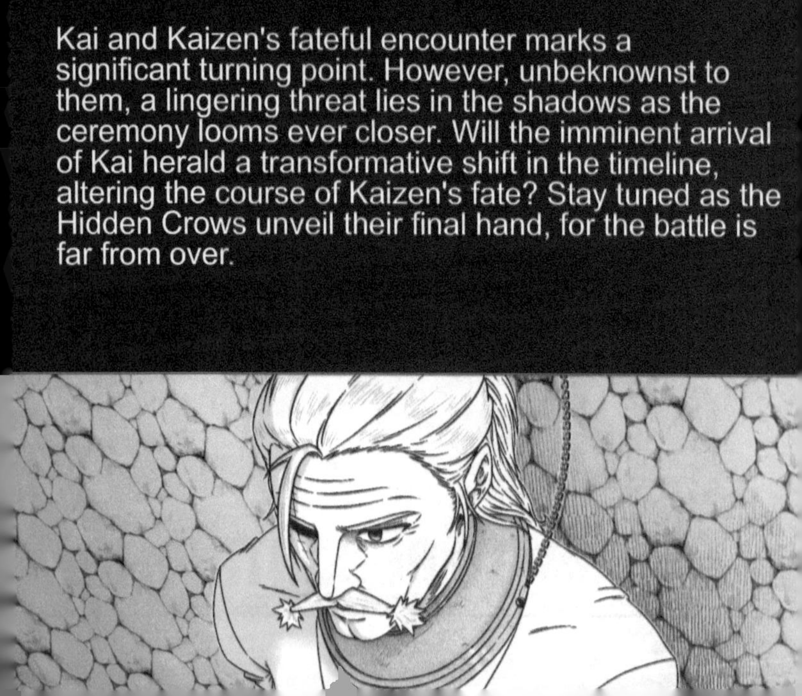

CONCEPT ART

Kai Sorashima

Kai's design hasn't changed much over the years, he has been refined as my art has evolved but the core of what I came up with has remained constant.

Kaizen Sorashima

Kaizen on the other hand
has had more drastic
changes. I like where I
eventually ended up but, it's
interesting looking back at
what could have been.

 SHEEZYCITIE

Love the composition and style of this piece! Every character is so expressive and I can tell that you understand these characters! Phenomenal work.

OKAHTZ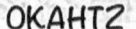

Definitely Kai's POV for sure. lol

MAJEK_ART

Great style, you really made this piece your own and I love how you gave Kai such an iconic pose!

THISMANGAOFMINE

Everything from
the angles to the
coloring is absolutely
stunning!

Ojay_252

I'm amazed how you
implemented blue
and gold into this
piece, Great work!

PSYCHO_BOI_M

The way you
adapted one of my
favorite scenes from
chapter 1 is definitely
something to admire!

YOU'RE READING IN THE WRONG DIRECTION!!

Uh-oh, you're starting on the wrong end of the comic, "In an amusing twist, while traditionally mangas are read from right to left in the original Japanese format, for the purpose of adapting it into an American format, where the norm is to read from left to right, this manga volume is working on cleverly reverse the reading direction, taking readers on a delightful journey through the captivating story, intricate illustrations, and dynamic action sequences, as they traverse the pages from left to right, immersing themselves in a fusion of Eastern and Western storytelling techniques, thus offering a fresh and unique experience for manga enthusiasts and newcomers alike."

-Editor

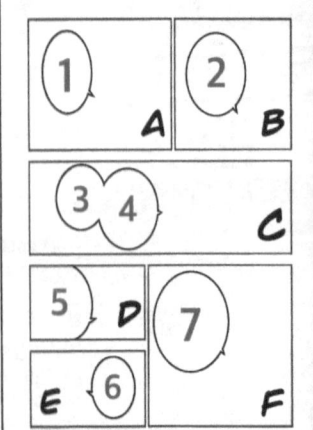

www.ingramcontent.com/pod-product-compliance
Lightning Source LLC
Chambersburg PA
CBHW030634120726
47904CB00006B/2151